Doddi the Dodo
GOES TO ORLANDO

Written by John Montgomery
Illustration by Julie Allen
Art Direction by Keith Hughes
Type Design by John Stadler

Everyone in Toledo, Ohio, thought **Doddi the Dodo** was a birdBrained yo-yo.

2

But **Doddi the Dodo** had moxie and mojo. She laughed it off, "Ha-ha, ho-ho!"

3

When winter came it was time to go
and fly South for the season in Orlando.
The Wind Started to blow

and before the birds could say,

"Where did Doddi GO?"

5

Doddi flew into a humongous, ginormous, voluminous tornado

6

Then Doddi fell to earth below.

8

She landed in the spray of a whale's blowhole.

9

She flew to northern Canada **where it WAS COld.**

Greetings from CANADA

She rocketed to England and said "**CHEERIO!**" Then, she took in a show.

Then she jetted to France
to see the City of Lights glo...

She zipped off to Spain,
to dance the flamenco

14

And went to the Swiss Alps to hear **an echo** echo echo

She caught the airflow to Italy
to say "Buon Giorno."

He flew solo to India **to take a photo.**

She played accordion in Moscow.

Greetings from
Moscow

She visited a dojo in a kimono and did judo in Tokyo.

She stopped by China to learn the lingo.

您好!

(Hello!)

She hopped with Australian kangaroos on a

JUMBO POGO.

CONGRATULATIONS.
YOU ARE NOW AT
AFRICAS HIGHEST POINT

She climbed Mt. Kilimanjaro and sailed down the Congo.

20

She dressed as a Pharaoh at the **Pyramids in Cairo.**

21

She ate right
so she could stay
on the go-go

to Acapulco, Soho, Monaco, Morocco, Oslo, Tierra del Fuego, Rio de Janeiro, Calico, Fresno, San Francisco, Reno, Durango, Waco, Idaho, Chicago, Ontario and Key Largo

23

and finally she flew to **guess where?**

ORLANDO

She said to her friends, "YO! GUESS WHERE I've been, bro?"

She told her stories and the flock cheered. "**Bravo, you're our hero.**"

"Won't you take us back to
ToLedo, Ohio,
when we go home...